TAIPAN
VS
BROWN

Also by Alexandria Blaelock

FICTION
That Love Nonsense
Taipan vs Brown
The Ghost and Ms Cox
Friends Like That
Weaving the Wildwood
Wolf vs Orb

SHORT STORY COLLECTIONS
Lovelorn, Lovestruck and Love at First Sight
Histories of Hayward Hall
Common or Garden Variety Heroes
Case Files of the Wilkinson National Detective Agency
Unavoidable Fates
Christmas Travesties
Five Faces of Felicia Clarke
Little Place Called Home
Security Directorate Dossiers volume 1
Security Directorate Dossiers volume 2

MS BLAELOCK'S BOOKS
Stress Free Dinner Parties
Signature Wardrobe Planning
Holistic Personal Finance
Minimally Viable Housekeeping
Planning a Life Worth Living

PICTURE BOOKS
Australia Felix

SELECTED SHORT STORIES

Alma's Grace	Life in the Security Directorate
Balancing the Book	Needy Bitch
Bygone Boyfriend	Onslaught at New Mir
Christmas Bonanza	Payton's Run
Dwennon's Despair	Secret Singer
Fate in Your Hands	Shining Star
Honeymoon Disaster	Ship in a Bottle
Kiss of Death	The Shadow Thieves
Lady of the Looking Glass	The Palace Hotel

TAIPAN VS BROWN

A GEORGIA GARSIDE PRIVATE EYE NOVELLA

ALEXANDRIA BLAELOCK

BlueMere Books
MELBOURNE, AUSTRALIA

For permission requests, please contact enquiries@bluemerebooks.com.

Ordering Information:
Discounts are available on quantity purchases. For details, contact orders@bluemerebooks.com.

Taipan vs Brown/Alexandria Blaelock
hardback ISBN: 978-1-922744-35-7
paperback ISBN: 978-1-922744-36-4
digital ISBN: 978-1-922744-37-1

Book Layout © BookDesignTemplates.com
Cover Art © Marie Žáková/Depositphotos

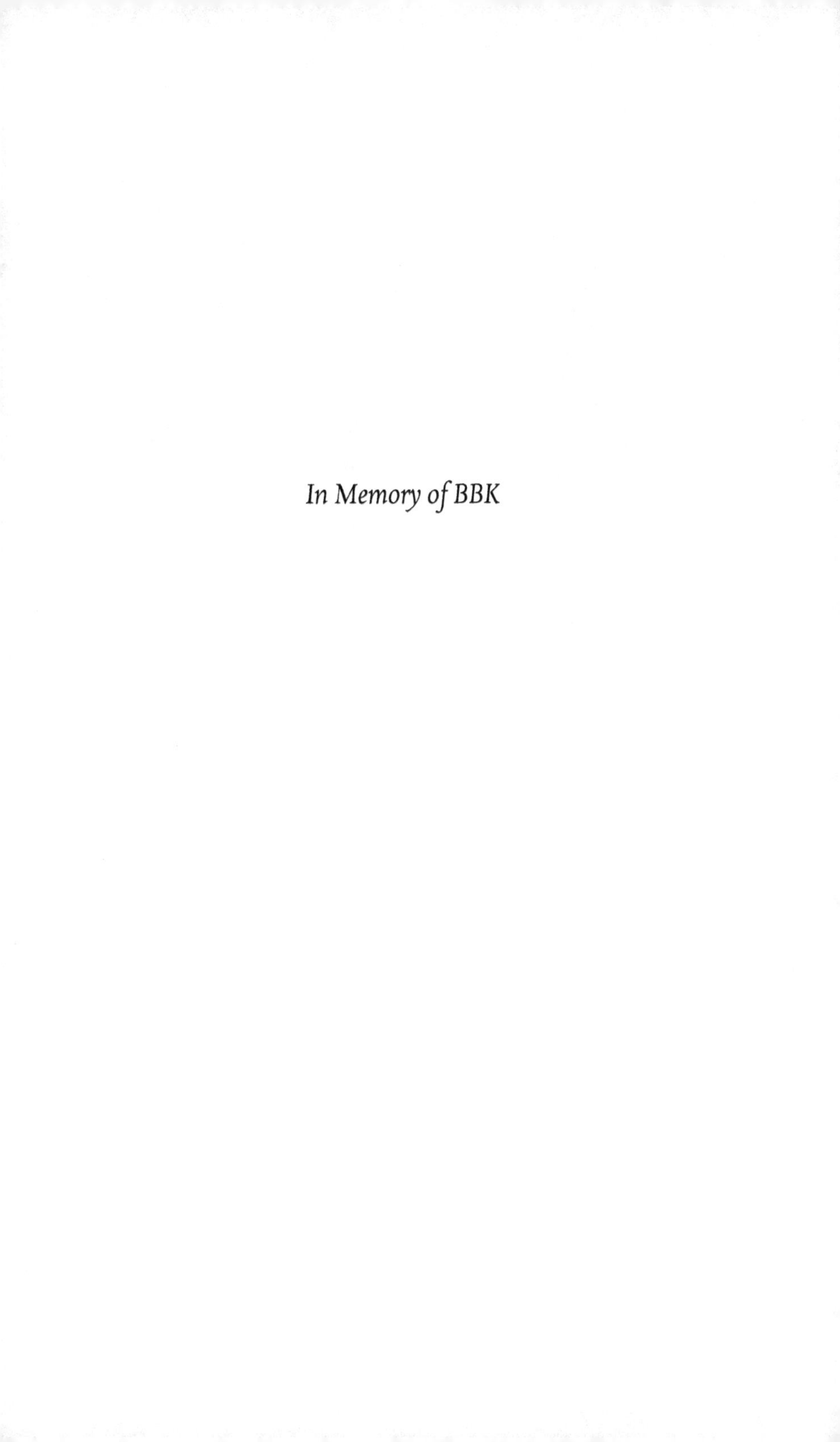

In Memory of BBK

The lion growls. Beware thy head.

– HOWARD PYLE

The story of how I came to find myself wedged under a desk, mere millimetres from its owner's legs is kind of funny in a kind of pathetically sad way.

It's because of a pretty lady (of course).

Or more particularly a seemingly rich damsel in distress.

Blackmailed by some cad without a conscience.

It was a pretty nice room as far as places to hide in go. And in my line of work, licensed Private Investigator for the poor and homeless, I've hidden in some pretty repulsive places.

For a start, it was a nice apartment on a high floor. Not the penthouse, but not far off it.

Nice luxurious hardwood floors laid over the concrete. But done on the cheap without levelling it before the insulating blanket went down.

Which is how I had enough warning to hide before the owner of said nice apartment and desk opened the study door.

Despite the nice deep burgundy paisley hall runner laid over it, the floor boards still creaked.

Then again, maybe they were going for aged authenticity.

I had about ten seconds to assess the mahogany desk, locked filing cabinet from which I had just retrieved an envelope, and a floor to ceiling bookshelf stacked with what looked like valuable first editions.

I ignored the burgundy velvet Victorian chaise longue and went for the desk.

Curled myself up like a pretzel and hid underneath it just as he opened the door.

Up until that moment I hadn't known who owned the cigar scented study, so hearing His voice was almost enough to make me lose my grip and fall out of my hiding place.

As his legs slid underneath me, and I smelled his herbal cologne and looked at his blue pinstriped crotch, I was sorely tempted to hang a little lower.

To brush against greatness.

So to speak.

Of course, it would've been curtains for me if He'd discovered me.

Might still be curtains, you never know.

I do know that if I'd known He was going to be in there so long, I'd've hidden in the narrow gap between the chaise and the wall.

As it was, I hung there for a couple a hundred years while He made a couple of calls.

And if the word got out He was betting black market on the horses...

Or that He maintained an apartment for a demanding young sugar baby...

In the same building of all places.

Well, I ask you.

Keeping the tramp in the same building had to be the dumbest idea ever. I mean when it came time to turf her out, she'd be no end of trouble.

Goes to show that however smart the big brain looks, the little brain between the legs is still in control.

You'd have to pay her good money or...

Take a more permanent solution.

I didn't want to think about how I'd never heard a whiff of scandal about him.

And I read the tabloids.

When He'd finally been called away by a man I assumed was the head of his security detachment, it took me a minute or two to drop to the floor.

While contortionism was my college party trick, it'd been a long while. And just like college football, contortionists can have career-ending injuries.

Enough said. It still haunts me.

I patted the envelope, safe in the internal pocket of my black top wondering what was inside it.

And how that pretty lady had known exactly where to find it.

But more importantly, how I was going to get out of the apartment when there were more people than Southern Cross Station out there.

So much for no one home.

I listened at the door, and hearing no sound, cracked it open a fraction.

Still nothing.

Hugged the wall as I crept down the corridor.

Avoided the creaky boards I'd tripped on my way in.

Ducked back into a doorway as a couple of guys stopped at the other end of the corridor to chat.

About their plans for the coming weekend when it was only Monday for fuck's sake.

I could barely think I was so hot with the jitters.

Just wanted to run screaming from the place.

Took all my hard-earned discipline to stay still and quiet until they moved on.

Step by slow step, back burning as it anticipated a bullet, I crossed the entry and made it out.

Easing the door closed behind me with the smallest of snicks as the lock engaged.

Sprinted down the corridor to the emergency stairs.

Bounded down two or three at a time for a couple of floors.

Paused to pull my hair back into a ponytail and straighten my clothes.

Picking up the apron and drinks tray I'd hidden in the fire hose cabinet, and walking back into the party I'd left to go rob the place upstairs.

No one seemed to notice my absence, and why would they?

Just the hired help.

And of course, my eyes widening, He was the first person I saw.

I hadn't realised he was so tall.

And much more attractive in person.

It took all my strength to lower my eyes and not touch the envelope resting against my belly.

I ferried drinks back and forth for a couple more hours.

Skin crawling the whole time, knowing he was there.

Picked up my coat, tucked my cash payment into my bag and left the building.

Paid twice for the same gig.

Well played if I do say so myself.

Right out the back door in the early hours of the morning like any good employee.

Paused to adjust my hair and powder my nose, and of course, look for suspicious characters in a tiny compact before leaving the staff entrance.

Seemed clear, but took the long way back to my office anyway.

When it comes to people, I reckon you've got the do-gooder Robin Hood types, and the go-getter Sheriff of Nottinghams.

I like to think I fall somewhere near the Robin Hood end of the spectrum.

Ethical, caring, working for the poor.

I even put cat food out for the strays in the alley behind my office, and when the big black fluffy one got sick, I took him to the vet.

Tried to keep him safe inside that first night, but he got out somehow, so I put a box out there for him to sleep in.

Now the Big Black Kitty is living like a king in a box castle right outside my door.

Now and again, he leaves a rat on the door mat (so to speak because there is no door mat) for me too.

I ain't complaining about that.

Though not yet desperate enough to eat one myself.

He still gets in and out.

Sits on my desk as I pretend to work.

That's not to say that the Sheriff wasn't doing his level best for King and country, trying to keep the peace as best he could against Robin of Lancaster, the criminal mastermind.

And failing dismally.

Or at least, having an inexperienced, and frankly useless public relations team.

He, on the other hand, was at the Sheriff of Nottingham end of the spectrum.

Captain of industry with political designs, spotless reputation, campaigning on law and order and family values.

Clearly with an experienced and reliable public relations team.

And presumably, a ruthlessly effective clean-up crew.

On the other side, a poor, but now I think about it, incredibly well-dressed pretty lady with a blackmail sob story.

A Goliath meets Goliath pro-wrestling prize fight.

My office (which I also sleep in because rents are expensive) is on the ground floor of a three-story building.

The rest of the building is leased out as offices for people walking the thin grey line between legit and not so legit.

Like the travel agent on the second floor who may or may not help fugitives escape justice by smuggling them out to other countries.

Or the beautician on the first, who administers cosmetic injectables when she's not licensed. Or insured.

And it's lucky I'm a minimalist because I sure as shit can't afford to be a maximalist.

My office is sparsely furnished, mainly from street dumps. My desk has three and a half legs, held up by a stack of old phone books.

So old you'd think they were yellow pages.

And a filing cabinet that takes a complicated one-two hip-shoulder movement to get it open and closed.

I got a particularly nice armchair, and the cat caught all the rats out of it one by one.

Way to go BBK.

I didn't turn the lights on case anyone was watching, but settled comfortably in the armchair.

Beer in one hand, homemade baccie (if you get my meaning) in the other, BBK licking his arse as he sat on the envelope on my desk.

I considered my options.

The Inland Taipan (AKA rich dude campaigning for a seat in the House of Reps) v the Eastern Brown (sob story pretty lady).

The point of the snake fight being, that it doesn't matter which one gets you, you're still dead.

Quicker by Taipan but probably more likely by Brown.

I balanced the beer on the floor; harder than you think after half a joint.

The good stuff because I'd done a good job.

And pulled the envelope out from under the cat.

Swaying under the influence as I opened it.

Realising I was so far up shit creek I didn't have a canoe.

Brown had come to me wearing a forest green felted beaver fedora with a feather in it. Pulled down at a rakish angle to conceal her face, but showing her blonde curls at the back.

Kind of like the German spies in the old war movies.

It was a perfect shade match for her forest green pencil skirt suit. And patent leather handbag...

I'd totted up the cost of her clothes, and been blinded by the dollar signs in my eyes.

Thinking Brown was desperate enough to cough up a couple of months' rent on my rat-infested office at any rate.

She was crying. Wouldn't look me in the eye. Twisted her wedding ring around her finger.

"It was a one-time thing," she sobbed. "I was drunk and angry just didn't think.

"We went up to his hotel room, and we... we... made love."

I doubt she made sweet, sweet love and I have no idea why that kind of woman can't call a fuck a fuck and get on with it.

Then again, maybe they don't fuck. Maybe that's what the sugar babes are for.

Anyhow, to cut the long, tear-stained story short, Taipan was blackmailing her and she wanted the negatives. Here was his address, probably in the filing cabinet.

I hadn't rolled my eyes when she was there, but I did now.

She'd turned out to be a bloody good actress.

But.

I couldn't believe I'd been so gullible.

Turns out women can be led astray by the little brain between their legs too.

Worse, the pretty woman who'd bamboozled me with flattery, flirtation, and a blackmail story, (or her representatives) were coming the next day to collect the "pictures."

Assuming they didn't turn up early.

The one single brain cell still synapsing in my head told me to get the hell out.

I grabbed the cat and slipped out the back.

Halfway down the alley when the building blew.

The blast sent me flying in one direction, and BBK cartwheeling in another.

I lay on the ground, looking up at the flames, and realised I still had the envelope and the joint.

But no wallet, no cash, no phone no identification.

In the battle of Taipan v Brown, Taipan was down by one.

But.

I couldn't lie about waiting for one or other of them to finish me off.

I had to move.

I'd've liked to think there were people I could rely on.

But I was in over my head.

To look for help would probably bring an even bigger mess of trouble down on their heads.

So, I was on my own.

I knew who Taipan was, but I had no idea who Brown might be.

Or whether she was behind the sting or just a bloody good actress hired to play the part.

In which case, I really hoped she was okay.

So, what the fuck was I to do with the envelope?

I couldn't exactly rock up and say, "hey mate, sorry, took this by mistake when I broke into your apartment. And by the way, you should really sack your security guy, he's seriously crap at his job."

I got up and staggered away, hoping no one had seen me.

Though even if someone local recognised me, they'd have thought I was working late.

And I couldn't tell whether that was a good thing or not.

I kept some stuff at the local gym, so I headed there to get cleaned up and put some fresh clothes on.

And wondered whether the security guy was in on it.

Maybe Taipan wasn't a bad man.

But I'd listened to those conversations.

Was it possible Brown was his sugar baby?

Had she decided to get her own back on him now her time was up?

Whichever way I looked at it, I couldn't settle.

Brown was clearly not the good guy if she'd tried to kill me.

And Taipan was not a good guy if he was the legitimate owner of the envelope.

Half my hair was burned off, so I hacked all the rest of the burnt bits off with some nail scissors.

It looked ridiculous, so I hacked some more to even it up.

So pissed off; it had taken years to get it that long.

Still, the pixie looked kind of cute for a home done job.

I considered burning the envelope as intended (though setting a bomb to dispose of it did seem overkill) but thought I might need it to guarantee my safe continuing existence.

But, then again, would I be safer without it?

I decided to turn the envelope in at the police station.

They'd open it and could decide what to do with it.

I begged an almond croissant and a latte from a friend of a friend at a local café and walked to the cop shop.

Took a seat as I waited my turn.

Watched one of them put up a wanted poster with my name on it.

For arson of all things.

I expect that'd be the Landlord's fault.

It wasn't that I never paid the rent, I just very rarely paid anything off the overdue.

Which I'd happily imagined doing when the building blew up.

Paid in full. I could see the red stamp pad ink of it draining away from me like a watercolour wash.

I waited a couple of moments then casually walked out.

Leaving the envelope behind on the seat.

Moseyed down the street, looking in the windows at the reflections of the people behind me.

Noticed a couple of guys tailing me.

Ducked into the twenty-four-hour supermarket.

Looked longingly at the racks of chips as I ran by.

And out the other side.

Cut across the railway tracks.

Saw a buck lying on the street.

Left it for someone who needed it more.

Pretty funny for someone who pretty much just lost everything they owned.

Full pelt out into the street beyond.

Down the street.

Left-hand turn.

Right-hand turn.

Into the rear entrance of a five-story apartment building.

Up to the exclusive roof-top garden with its excellent views of the surrounding local streets.

Accessible only to a very few non-residents who knew how to get into it.

Knowledge I'd come by on a previous job.

Paused to catch my breath as I stood under a tree looking out.

No sign of pursuit.

But no time to be complacent.

I had to come up with a plan.

But just for a moment, I let myself breathe.

Ugly deep gasping breaths.

Looking up and allowing myself to be distracted by tiny birds flitting from tree to tree, listening to them chirp.

Pretending everything was tickety-boo.

That I wasn't running in fear for my life.

Imagining I'd come to buy one of the apartments on the top floor. The closest I'd ever get to luxury.

I—

2

When I woke up, I was lying on a scratchy grey couch in a strange room with white painted walls.

Sunlight streamed through a gap in the yellow floral printed curtains.

It smelled faintly of lavender.

And vomit.

In front of the couch sat a coffee table with a clear plastic jug of a liquid that looked a lot like water and an upside-down glass on a tray.

I remained still, holding my breath, listening to the silence.

It seemed like a guest room come study kind of room.

With flatpack beech-effect furniture.

And wall-to-wall cream shag carpet.

More luxurious than the fifth story apartments I'd been kidnapped from, but not as luxurious as Taipan's.

I mean he had real furniture for one thing. Possibly antiques. Quite tasteful.

I wasn't tied up.

So that was a nice surprise.

I got up to look out the window; the quality of light looked about lunchtime.

Which partly explained the grumbly sensation in my tummy.

The city spread about around me, so I had an idea where I was. Could have been Taipan's building again.

And so far as I could tell from that far up, there were a lot of people out on the street.

I found a bathroom, splashed my face with water and drank out of the tap.

I figured it was more complicated to mess with a bathroom than a jug.

I heard a key in the door.

Pride would not let me hide in the bathroom.

I was not a kid anymore.

And it was too late to find somewhere else.

I had to brazen it out.

Heart thumping, I took up a defensive position in the hallway.

Knees slightly bent, ready to spring.

Hands on hips as if I owned the place.

Taipan opened the door.

Paused for a fraction of a second when he saw me, then kept walking until he was close enough to touch me.

Close enough I wanted to back away from him.

As it was, my lip may have curled, and I may have swayed back a little despite my resolution.

After all, he was very tall, and I am not, and I had to crane my neck to look up at him.

But sometimes brave faces are the hardest things to put on.

Like that time just after I'd moved into my filthy flea pit of an office.

I was dancing around, phone on the table, earbuds screwed in. Eighties hits on the playlist.

When I heard a voice that could etch glass, "so this is where you're hiding out now Georgia Garside."

I froze, John Travolta impersonation wasted on my nemesis.

I took a moment to evoke the Ice Queen then turned.

"Mother," I said.

She was of course immaculately dressed. Now that I think of it, a lot like Brown.

Except her white gloves were stained by the door handle.

Fascinating she'd come alone and touched the door herself.

Mother, like Taipan, is a go-getter.

She married into the family and keenly feels the responsibility of protecting the wealth and reputation of the Garside name.

Despite my father's lack of the same.

I suppose Mother feels she needs to prove herself to Gran and is, therefore, more protective.

Hilarious given Gran married into the family too.

I suspect Mother will never receive Gran's warrant of approval.

But it's quite possible Mother feels the disappointment of a daughter run wild even more keenly.

Especially when Gran gleefully supports me in my endeavours to live my own life.

Separately.

Maybe Gran's the reason why Mother made me sign the document renouncing my family membership.

With all the rights and responsibilities pursuant.

"Georgia I really don't understand why you won't give up this nonsense and come home."

I sighed. The sad truth was she really didn't.

She thought it was a passing fad. Like ballet or ballroom dancing.

Something else I'd grown out of.

You remember I said I was a do-gooder?

Go-getters just don't get do-gooders, whereas do-gooders know all about go-getters.

Anyhow.

Taipan held his hands up and said, "I am unarmed."

As if that was some kind of reassurance.

I narrowed my eyes.

He already knew I had no weapons.

Not that it's legal to carry them here anyway, even before the Gangland War. Certainly didn't stop the wave of tit-for-tat murders in the criminal underworld.

So.

Imagine for a moment, the string bikini-clad ladies walking around the wrestling ring holding placards with the scores up for the audience.

Taipan one, Brown one.

Dead heat.

It was as much as I could do not to go nuts and beat the crap out of him.

Technically it wasn't his fault.

He hadn't set this whole situation up.

But his actions had led me to this point.

"You can relax," he held an envelope up, "I have the photos."

And I did relax.

Just for a moment.

Such was the timbre of his charming voice.

Then I remembered I had exited the frying pan and was now well and truly in the fire.

And grew even more tense.

As you do when you come across a poisonous snake.

But remained still.

Mostly expressionless.

Eyes lazily looking for an escape that didn't involve running straight through him and out the door.

Almost crying when I realised there was next to nothing I could do.

I wasn't upset *per se*, more like frustrated.

I'd struggled for years to get out from under Mother's yoke.

I'd hidden under his desk less than the twenty-four hours ago, and I'd already fallen into the palm of his hand.

My life had gone to shit.

Mother could learn a thing or twenty from him.

I folded my arms across my chest and scowled.

"I just want to check one thing with you before I let you go."

I was pretty sure his version of letting me go involved a window and a fall with a long drop.

He took a phone out of the breast pocket of his immaculately tailored charcoal grey, presumably fine merino wool jacket, tapped a couple of times and showed me a picture of Brown.

"Is this the woman who hired you?"

For a moment I debated the wisdom of not confirming his surmise with myself.

Then nodded.

He smiled a thin-lipped straight smile and put the phone away.

And clasped his hands together behind his back.

"You can go now," he said.

"Just like that?"

"Just like that."

"What's the catch?" I asked.

"No catch. You can walk away and never hear from me again."

I nodded.

Can, can, can.

As though I had the power to walk through him.

Not to mention that his body was telling me something else.

Mainly because it hadn't stepped away from the door.

"Or?"

"You can help me get my revenge."

I rolled my eyes.

That right there was more or less exactly what I was expecting.

There was no walking out that door without that fall.

"All you have to do, is plant this envelope in her apartment."

All you have to do.

For fuck's sake, "all you have to do," is never as quick or easy or simple as it sounds.

"And that's all?"

"That's all."

"I don't know where she lives."

"I'll give you the address."

And then he gave me the key.

3

So I found myself once more, inside his building.

Listening to a door on an apartment that wasn't mine.

No sound.

Except my wildly beating heart.

I put the key in the lock and turned it.

And was immediately greeted by a small snarling ball of white fur with beige teeth.

You'd think he could've mentioned it.

But perhaps he thought I deserved it.

And maybe Brown had timed her extraction so I'd get caught too.

Thankfully the fluff ball was only about calf-high.

Though very opinionated.

"Hello precious," I said.

The snarling wall of fur rolled on its back and exposed its male belly.

I gave it a good rub.

He cycled his legs in ecstasy.

If only everyone I met was that easy to get along with.

"Good boy."

I stepped over him and moved on.

He followed.

I'm sure it was a nice enough apartment as far as they go, though not much character if you ask me.

Clean white walls and carpets, sparsely furnished with white leather furniture.

I suppose the white dog hair wouldn't be an issue.

I was detecting a theme.

And wondering who chose the décor; Brown or Taipan.

Plus, I was getting the idea the apartment wasn't worth the hassle of the attached sugar-daddy.

You know what I mean.

A bit like the dog.

Come when called. Do what you're told. Don't bite the hand that feeds you.

And thinking again, I suppose that's what Mother's done.

All her adult life.

Though she gets to enjoy it when Dad's attention wanders, knowing he might never touch her with passion, but he's never going to leave her.

Almost enough for me to...

No, not really.

Anyhow, I got the impression Taipan was trying to divest Brown, but she wasn't taking the hint.

As I looked for somewhere to hide the envelope, I idly wondered if he'd found her replacement yet.

I didn't open the envelope.

And I have no idea what was in it.

Nor do I want to know.

Just left it in the middle of a bunch of papers on her tiny white desk.

As if she'd dropped it there but not got back to it before the other stuff piled up.

Score check please.

Cue the string bikini-clad ladies holding placards with the scores: Taipan two, Brown one.

My fatal undoing came as I was walking back through the lounge.

Took one last look through the plate glass windows over the city and down to the ocean.

Rudely interrupted by something fat and wide like a Pelikan Souveran M1000 fountain pen poking in my back.

Or a gun.

Honestly, I'm losing my touch if she could sneak up on me that easily.

"What are you doing here?" she asked.

I struggled for a moment to come up with something witty to say.

Then gave up.

"Just wondered what your place looked like."

She poked me again.

"I don't believe you."

I turned and disarmed her.

"Well," I said, "you did just blow my house up."

Just enough time to see a dark ponytail as she swept a slap at me.

She laughed, "you were supposed to be in it."

She had the kind of laugh that was infectious.

I found myself grinning.

And wondered, could we have been friends in different circumstances?

I grasped the enormous pen by its fat barrel and blocked the slap with my forearm.

"You've got room," I said, "I thought I might move in."

She aimed a kick, "you can't afford me."

I twisted away.

Slapping her ankle bone with the pen as I rotated.

"Bitch," she yelped.

I smiled grimly.

Was going for her foot.

Came round the full circuit to jab at her face with the pen.

She swayed back, "face is off-limits."

Over-correcting, she took two steps back.

I pointed the pen at her.

Barely pausing to wonder whether the blond or dark was the wig.

"Yeah, I get it. Your face is your fortune."

Not a Pelikan; Visconti.

Nice.

But nowhere near as good as a fan for distraction.

"You'd better believe it," she said, sweeping a kick my way.

She wasn't a bad fighter *per se*, probably quite good in the sense of classes and tournaments.

But she took a classroom learned fraction of a second delay between moves that meant she'd be absolute shit at street fighting.

"He's mine, you stay away from him," she said.

How tiresome. How predictable. How pathetic.

As if He was anyone's except his own.

And if she couldn't hold his attention, she clearly wasn't what he was looking for.

I rapped her knuckles with the pen.

She squeaked and redoubled her attack.

Allowed her to herd me towards the door and out.

Pocketed the pen and bolted down several flights of stairs.

Elevator to the basement.

Out via the shopping mall that shared the car park.

Once more checking the window reflections for followers as I walked.

I can't say as how I've learned a lot in my life, but I *have* learned it's unwise to get between a woman and her meal ticket.

Doesn't matter whether it's a boyfriend or a fuck buddy or a sugar daddy.

Some women take it a little too seriously.

Others take it a lot too seriously

Granted Taipan looked a generous meal ticket.

And I was fairly sure I'd heard he wasn't married.

Unless he was doing a Mr Rochester.

Which didn't seem likely.

As I said, I read the tabloids and they're usually right on top of that kind of stuff.

So perhaps Brown was angling for the position of wife.

He didn't seem the kind to be pinned down so easily.

Going by my monthly hot chocolate and hot water bottle assisted romance movie marathons, she was going about it the wrong way.

Instead of clinging to him, she should be scorning him.

Urggghhhh.

Enough of that.

I ran a complicated route between clothes, bag and shoe shops.

Partly to confound anyone foolish enough to follow me.

Partly because I needed new clothes.

As I got changed Brown's fountain pen fell on the floor.

I looked at it.

It was a nice pen.

I could leave it behind in the store. Or drop it in at a Police Station. Or give it to Taipan.

And then I thought about keeping it. Because it didn't seem likely Brown was going to pay my invoice.

More likely laugh like a comic book villain as she scrunched it into a ball and threw a three-pointer in the bin.

Then again, I didn't have a printer or any invoices thanks to her.

And I reckoned it was worth a couple of grand at least. I could pawn it. Or sell it.

Or just keep it.

I shoved it in my new pocket.

Yes, I discounted the new gear.

I did feel bad about that and made a mental note to send the money later.

Then exited out the other side of the mall into the train station.

Where I jumped the turnstile and crisscrossed through a couple of railway lines as I made my way back to what remained of my office.

4

I was delighted to find BBK was okay.

He saw me coming, ran down the alley and jumped into my arms.

Something missed me.

Weirder than that, he climbed up my shirt and draped himself around my neck.

Even weirder still, I let him.

I carried him as I wandered about kicking at stuff on the ground.

Looking for my cash box.

There was no doubt about it.

The building was a write-off.

A pile of smoking rubble.

In the middle, a filing cabinet rising from a small lake.

My filing cabinet.

I guess they knew how to make them in those days.

Gave it the old hip and shoulder and it opened up to reveal a bunch of ashes.

Stirred the ashes just in case something had survived, but it crumpled to dust.

No cash box.

Not that there would've been much in it.

I had no idea what I was going to do.

Until I saw my landlord.

And remembered the wanted posters.

And wondered if I could even get my hands around his thick neck.

Then sighed.

Wouldn't do to murder him right off the bat.

The shady git approached me with his hands up.

If I had been the gun-carrying kind that wouldn't have saved him.

Probably just as well I'm not licensed to carry.

Though I was exhausted, and that saved him from the threat of physical violence.

"I'm sorry," he said.

I cocked one eyebrow.

"Some woman called the police and told them specifically she saw you light the fire."

That narrowed my list of suspects to Brown and Mother.

"I told the cops there was no way you'd do that because you practically lived here."

Ah. So he'd noticed.

"What are you going to do now?" I asked.

"Dunno. I'm too old for this shit."

This shit being the rubble.

Wasn't sure whether he meant the drama or being the crap-arse property manager he'd been.

I nodded.

"Anyhow, the insurance'll barely cover the clean-up let alone reconstruction."

I nodded again.

He shrugged and kicked some melted thing, probably my cash box, on the ground as he said "them's the breaks, eh?"

I grunted noncommittally.

"I'm still gonna need the rent due, plus the arrears."

Obviously.

"I'll get it to you as soon as I can. Bearing in mind there's nothing left."

His turn to grunt.

We looked over the wreckage for a minute or two.

"What will you do now?" he asked.

I scrubbed my head with both hands, accidentally wedging BBK's head between mine and my arm.

I'd forgotten he was there.

"I don't know. Set up somewhere else I suppose."

"Yeah, best to get right back on the horse," he said.

I wondered exactly what kind of horse he thought I'd fallen off.

"Right."

"Well, good luck Georgie," he said, holding out his hand.

It would have been churlish to refuse to shake his hand.

Especially as he hadn't tried to kill me.

And didn't say anything more about the money I owed him.

He turned and picked his way through the remains of his building.

I reached up to scratch BBK's chest.

"What do you want to do BBK?"

He rubbed his cheek along mine and started purring.

No fucking help at all.

Typical male.

5

I joined the evening commuters, catching the train in the direction of Gran's place.

BBK wouldn't let go, so I took him along for the ride.

Now I expect that when I said Gran's place, you imagined a big, old and imposing mansion. Or perhaps a new ultra-modern mansion.

The kind of place wealthy beyond imagining people live in exclusive gated enclaves.

But remember, I told you she married into the family?

Gran's house is in fact, a tiny three-bedroom, one-bathroom suburban weatherboard home. White walls, eucalypt green tin roof.

Fairly traditional layout; three bedrooms down one side, separated from the kitchen, dining, lounge down the other side. Combined bathroom and laundry in the lean to out the back.

The style is commonly referred to as a Bullet house, so-called because it's possible to shoot a bullet from the front door through the back without hitting anyone.

The house is on a large block mind you. Framework of trees to shade the house. Lawn and flowers at the front, fruit trees and vegetable beds at the back. She still does all the gardening herself.

Did you know that the term orchard relates to the pattern and spacing of the trees, and not the number?

Gran makes her own jams and preserves, pretty much the same as her Gran did. She gave me the book of schedules and recipes, updated by her mother and Gran herself.

The cottage is as cute as a tiny wooden button shaped like a mouse with a tiny leather tail and ears, and tiny plastic whiskers.

It's the house Gran grew up in.

The house she and her new husband lived in with her parents when his family disinherited him over his choice of wife.

And the house her parents left her, because they didn't want her to be dependent on his capricious family.

Well thought out if you ask me.

Gramps would've been perfectly happy to stay in that little cottage for his lifetime, working at his job in the insurance office.

Only he was the only Garside with any business sense. His parents were forced to reconcile if they wanted to see their business empire thrive.

Which it did for another generation; I think Dad's pretty much pissed it all away so I'd be amazed if there was anything left for anyone else.

Shame really, mother could've been born for running the business.

Anyhow, I walked up the long, pine-shaded drive, BBK still draped around my shoulders.

Napping.

And the closer I got to the cottage, the more troubled I became.

It had been a tumultuous day...

Two days?

It had been a tumultuous time and all I wanted to do was take a hot bath and sleep for about a month.

Maybe six weeks.

And eat a crap-tonne of Gran's sticky ginger cake.

But I had the sense the Taipan v Brown prize fight was a long way from over.

What with having been caught in the middle.

And lost everything.

I wondered what they could possibly do next.

To me mainly, but also the people I cared about.

And everyone else in the fall out zone.

And seeing as Brown came to me first, what she might do to up the ante.

Relatedly, what the two of them had already done to fuck up everyone else.

My thoughts circled my brain like goldfish.

I really needed to get some shut-eye.

And then I had some thinking to do - both long and short-term, seeing as I'd lost my business and my not exactly legal residence.

"Bubba Gee!" Gran squealed, "I wasn't expecting you today? And my goodness what have you done to your hair?"

And that was all it took.

As she opened her arms, my lips started wobbling and a few tears leaked from my eyes as I tried to brave it out in Gran's hug.

Forgetting about BBK again.

I reached up to my shoulder to grasp his foot. He flexed his claws in my hand, and for a moment, I felt I could do anything.

Then he slipped down my back and sauntered off to investigate the garden.

Particularly the flock of brightly coloured parrots trying to get at the netted citrus trees.

He took my energy with him and tiredness rolled over me like a wave.

Gran dropped her arms, "You look dead on your feet."

I remember her being bigger, but now she's a tiny bird-like creature. Especially in the rounded stomach department.

With long white hair she pulls back into a ponytail because she thinks she looks younger than in a bun.

I nodded.

I love Gran, I really do, but she's an inordinate gossip. And the thought of filling her in on all the details exhausted me.

"Tea first," she pursed her lips as she looked at me, "good strong Assam I think."

I followed her as she briskly walked through to the old-fashioned kitchen out the back. She was cooking lemon marmalade on the blue enamel wood stove.

My mouth watered.

Not quite soon enough, she put a steaming mug of black tea in front of me, along with a thick slice of ginger cake.

Patting my hand as she moved away to make the same for herself.

It was exactly what she'd offered when I got beaten up at that stupid exclusive girls' school. Didn't make it hurt any less, but I felt like I'd earned it.

I'd managed to hold off the tears until I sat down.

A bit like when you're really drunk and manage not to throw up until you get home. Usually either the minute before or the minute after you shut the door, you lose control.

A single tear rolled down my face.

Soon joined by another.

And another.

And then a torrent more.

Gran stirred another spoon of sugar into my tea.

Then patted my back and said, "there, there."

She was just carrying a box of tissues to the table when the world went nuts.

I heard a crash.

From the front of the house.

Followed by another.

And another.

And then tinkling.

More crashes.
And thudding.
As whatever it was hit the floor.
Or walls.
Within fractions of a second it was moving down the side of the house.
Brain finally connected the dots.
Just enough time to pull Gran to the floor.
Bullets raked the back of the house.
A car revved its engine.
Skidding on the lawn as it rounded the corner.
Up the bedroom side of the house.
"Gran, stay here."
Crouch ran up to the hall to get details of the car.
There was no way I was letting this go.
To coin a phrase, now it was personal.
Hadn't noticed the dark drawing in.
Kept to the shadows.
Just in case.
Driver did a couple of burnouts.
Over Gran's flower beds!
White utility.
Generic tradie style.
Built-in steel tool box in the tray.
No obvious sign of the shooter.
Couldn't see the license plate clearly.
Maybe an oh.
Perhaps an eight

Couldn't see more.

Not clearly enough to be sure.

The ute stopped at the street.

I heard a whumpf and turned in time to see the ute go up in flames.

Saw two men running.

Heard the wail of sirens.

I had been foolish.

Anyone with a bit of computer sense could look me up.

Once you found me...

Wouldn't take long to find the rest of my family, our addresses, and probably a good deal of our schedules.

All that stupidity about looking for tails and changing trains.

And all anyone had to do was bloody well look us up on the internet.

I threw my hands up and kicked the wall.

As much as I didn't like Mother, she was still family.

Had to warn her.

Turned and walked into Gran.

"I'm guessing you shouldn't be here when the Police arrive," she said.

Shoving a wad of cash into my hand and placing a large, dark plaid overcoat around my shoulders.

I shrugged into it, "I can't leave you on your own."

She smiled a straight lipped smile as she smoothed the coat's shoulders over mine, "people don't shoot up old lady's houses for no reason. I'll be fine."

"But—"

She crushed the air out of my lungs, "you'd better get going. The Police will be here soon."

"Okay, but tell them it was a white ute and the license plate contained an oh and an eight."

She nodded.

I hugged her again and took off, keeping to the shadows.

I was on the run again.

In a hideous, but warm coat.

I shoved the money in my pocket and headed to the station.

Paid for my train ticket.

Score check: Taipan two, Brown two.

Tie break.

6

About an hour later I arrived at my parents' home. Their house is probably almost exactly what you imagined Gran's house might be like.

Only a more tasteless pastiche of styles and features is hard to imagine. Art Deco roof lines with glass balustrades. Queen Anne towers with coloured tiles. Prison like security screens.

Took two trains, a tram and a short walk to get there.

Plenty of time to rehearse the hundreds of ways to tell her she had to take care.

Thinking she was right to make me sign that paper.

She opened the door and looked at me. "You can't stay here."

I took a deep breath and let it out. I had hoped to avoid an immediate argument.

"Gran's house got shot up."

"I know, she called to let me know you were coming."

She looked at me expectantly. I struggled to know where to start.

"They bombed my office...

"Then they...

"But he said it was over..."

Mother sighed theatrically.

"Why don't you start at the beginning."

So, right there on the doorstep, I started with Brown's visit, the story she told me, the theft from Taipan's office.

Mother's eyes bulged.

Then the bombing, planting something in Brown's place, Gran's place.

She put her hands on her hips, "would any of this have happened if you'd played nice and stayed at that marketing company?"

I looked at my feet and shook my head.

"Wait here," she said shutting the door.

Loud.

I wondered if doors could be manufactured to sound dismissive.

It didn't seem very long before the security light went out leaving only the street light leaking through the large, privacy guaranteeing leafy trees for illumination.

I jumped around, partly to keep warm, and partly hoping to trigger the lights.

They did not come on again.

Not even when she finally opened the door.

"You need to go under the radar for a while, so here's a pre-paid mobile," she looked up for a moment before turning her gaze on me, "I think there's fifty dollars on it."

My jaw dropped as she offered it to me.

"This is the key to my *pied-a-terre* in Treasury Place, and this," she held out a bank wrapped pack of twenty-dollar notes, but didn't let it go when I grasped the other end of it, "is a loan, not a gift."

I smiled, that sounded more like Mother.

"Call me in a couple of days. I'll see what I can find out from the Gossip Club."

The Gossip Club was my derogatory name for her Bridge Club, made up of other well-to-do ladies with too much time on their hands.

"Thank you Mother."

"Pfft," she said waving her hand dismissively, "if anyone's going to kill you, they'll have to get in line after me."

I grinned, but before I could say anything more, she cupped my cheek in her hand and said, "try not to get killed before I see you next."

And gently closed the door on me.

Which smarted a little, but she'd been way more generous than I'd expected.

7

Mother's apartment turned out to be, well, nice. Large and spacious in a lovely old period property.

Comfortable. Services more than adequate.

I took a long, long, scalding hot shower, dressed in some of Mother's jeans and a t-shirt that weren't repulsive.

Made myself a snack of instant ramen. Not something I thought I'd ever see in the same place as her.

Opened a bottle of beer and drank half of it in the first swallow.

Feeling almost human, I put the tv on and opened the box of a brand-new laptop.

While I waited for it to boot up, I wondered how long Mother had to prepare for my arrival, and who did the actual work of it.

Probably the building *concierge* service.

Presumably well paid to be discreet.

I opened an incognito window on a search engine and opened a new account with a complementary email.

Then started an in-depth search on Taipan.

Who did not have a wife hidden in the attic, just a succession of pretty (sugar baby) girlfriends.

None of them lasting more than a couple of months.

By which method I found out Brown's identity.

So, I did a deep search on her. Very active on social media with the usual "look at me I'm so pretty" pictures and sentiments.

Nothing to suggest she had a brain let alone was a psychopath, though it was possible to infer she was a reckless risk-taker who wasn't over fond of the truth.

Not altogether different to the opinion I'd already made of her.

But as I kept searching further and further back, it seemed she was also clever, manipulative, and had been in trouble with the law before.

Though so far as I could tell, she hadn't blown up any buildings previously.

And technically, she still hadn't - that she knew when it would go off did not mean she'd laid the bomb, or even that she'd caused the bomb to be there in the first place.

But that she knew, and didn't warn anyone (let alone me) was highly suggestive of culpability.

She'd been involved in fights.

In one instance, had cut a woman's face because the woman had been drunk and flirted with Brown's boyfriend of the minute.

Brown was stone-cold sober at the time.

Sliced to the bone and laughed as she was dragged away.

If the woman hadn't had a good plastic surgeon...

So perhaps this was evidence of an inability to distinguish between right and wrong.

Certainly no signs of remorse or empathy.

And no regard for the rights of others.

Which definitely counted as socially irresponsible behaviour.

Probably a tendency to lie.

And not just to me.

Often.

Probably about everything.

To everyone.

I deeply regretted getting involved with her.

Though how was I to know?

And who's to say that had I said no, I wouldn't have been in the middle of it anyway.

Why had she chosen me? I doubted it was random happen-stance.

We didn't move in the same circles, though Brown didn't seem to have a circle.

Would it be easier to kill some lowlife than someone known and respected?

Or god help me, had I offended her at some point?

I couldn't remember having met her, let alone think of a time when I might have said or done something to annoy her.

And then it occurred to me that I was still thinking of her as a blonde, though I'd seen her with dark and light hair. Scrolled back through the pictures to find she was predominantly blonde.

Thought back to time served at St Brigid's School for Girls where I was teased so mercilessly for my bad acne, I'd been driven to seek help a dermatologist.

And teased for my crooked teeth thus the orthodontist.

Searched for the school and discovered someone had scanned the yearbooks and made them accessible online.

I skimmed through them but didn't see anyone who looked like a proto-Brown.

Had something similar happened to Brown? At some other school?

Or was I still missing something at St Brigid's?

One day, when I wasn't trying to save my own life, I had to work out some kind of screening criteria to save me from psychos.

Perhaps open my investigations to people who could afford more than barter with homegrown tomatoes (though they were delicious).

Or clothes alteration (though I did like to be well dressed).

Or a lifetime of free dry-cleaning when I had something decent in the wardrobe (though that might still be handy).

Would that be better or worse than coming to some sort of arrangement with Mother over an allowance?

No doubt in exchange for certain kinds of more "appropriate" activities.

Like staying neat and clean and attending one thousand dollars a plate charity dinners.

I would draw the line at The Gossip Club.

I sighed.

And went back to Taipan.

Trying to gauge when he took up with Brown; how he'd met her, and how that impacted on his business.

When I looked at the stock market, shares in his company were on a downward trend.

Since about the time he met her.

Can't have been coincidence.

So, what was she up to?

Was it as simple as becoming Mrs Taipan, or was it something more along the lines of KAOS; hell-bent on world domination?

Was there some industrial secret in particular she was trying to get at?

I had to bear in mind she was still a bloody good actress.

Who had tried to kill me.

Twice!

And you know what they say; fool me once, shame on you. Fool me twice, shame on me.

Despite the tv news blaring in the background.

No matter how unlikely a mention of my case was.

Or how much I wanted to hear what a journalist might deduce about it.

Or what they might say about an old lady's house in the outer suburbs being shot up.

I found my eyes closing.

The weight of my head increasing.

And my chin hitting my chest as I fell asleep cross-legged on the couch over the open laptop.

Like I said. It had been a tumultuous time.

8

The next morning dawned bright and clear.

And seeing as I hadn't shut the curtains, early.

I attempted to ease my aching neck with a hot shower.

And then a slow walk to a café for the largest latte I could get. Along with the largest toasted BLT.

Sat outside to watch the commuters scurrying by.

Relaxing as much as I could.

Trying to give my brain a moment to catch up with the rest of me.

Maybe even get a little ahead.

I wasn't helping myself much.

Probably would've been better going back to bed for more rest.

But while my body was dead tired, my brain was all over the place.

Walked the long way back to Mother's apartment, hoping that had been enough.

As I walked back into the building, the big guy in the black suit behind the desk called my name, "Uh, Miss Garside."

I approached the desk, "yes?"

"Your mother left a package for you, if you wouldn't mind waiting, I'll get it for you."

Obviously, she hadn't left it personally.

A short time later he was back, reverently carrying a long, flat white box wrapped in a large red ribbon.

I thanked him.

The box was an awkward carry for a woman of my size, no doubt made to impress others.

Got it back to the apartment, pulled off the ribbon and folded back the tissue paper to find an evening dress.

The fabric was magnificent. Shot silk - blue or purple depending on how the light hit it.

I carefully pulled it out and held it up against my body.

I didn't loathe it.

In fact, I quite liked it.

It was plainly styled; semi-fitted, high round neck, elbow-length sleeves, ankle-length skirt; not too tight and not too wide.

It looked like the kind of dress I'd be able to run and fight in, as well as dance and scale small mountains.

I patted down the sides - no pockets.

On the one hand, no disturbances to the line, on the other, nowhere to stuff tissues. Or carry phones.

And on the bottom of the box, wrapped in a black velvet shoe bag; matching low-heeled shoes.

The combination was perfect, fancy, but not too fancy.

Something I could run in if I needed to.

For an instant, I hated Mother with a passion.

Not entirely clear whether I was a guest or a body guard.

Which I am also licensed for.

But convinced either way, the fancy evening she had planned would cost me.

The dress came with a card:

12:00 Lunch at Mirelle

14:00 Kireina Salon

20:00 Royal Hotel

And attached to the card, an overblown gilt-edged invitation to a dinner supporting prostate cancer.

I sighed.

Lunch and beauty treatments - whatever was happening at the Royal Hotel was really going to cost me.

And then I started wondering what she'd found out.

And who we'd be meeting.

At the appointed time, I sat in the restaurant, nursing a lemon, lime and bitters with a generous slug of vodka.

Probably not the wisest thing to drink.

On the one hand, I needed my wits about me, on the other, I needed something to take the edge off time spent with Mother.

And on my brain addled third hand, my brain was addled.

Did you know addled also refers to an egg that doesn't produce a viable chick?

Or more probably, *originally* referred to an egg that didn't produce a viable chick.

Addled egg.

Funny.

I expected Mother to spend the hour harassing me about my life choices.

No boyfriend. No job. No visible signs of support.

Home and business blown up in the course of said business.

But she talked about her rose garden and the flower arranging course she was doing.

That Gran hadn't lost much in the way of vegetables, but the fruit trees might not survive the rain of bullets.

And BBK was ok!

I'd forgotten about BBK.

But so relieved he'd survived the second attempt on my life.

He'd moved partway indoors with Gran.

Who thought he was adorable. As opposed to the hard-bitten street fighting tiger I knew him to be.

So all in all, an hour and a half with an attractive stranger who looked a lot like my mother.

Weird.

She left me to enjoy Kireina Salon on my own.

Also weird.

Perhaps she didn't want to push her luck.

I watched as they cut and coloured my hair layering three different colours of dye. Once that was washed out, they applied a treatment and wrapped my head in cling wrap.

Snored my way through the full-body salt crystal exfoliation.

Woke up briefly for the full leg and bikini wax!

I'd forgotten how painful they are.

And wondered who Mother thought I'd be seducing.

Napped again during the balancing and repair facial, hydrating body wrap, and deluxe mani-pedi with purple-blue polish.

Mother must have specified exactly what she wanted to look like at the other end.

Back to the chair for a wash and style.

And a surprisingly dramatic interpretation of a subtle make-up application. With smoky dark purple eye-shadow.

I kind of liked it.

Feeling pampered, rejuvenated and restored when they spat me out five hours later.

Sending the bill to Mother.

I walked back to the apartment.

Where a small plate of delicious sandwiches and a thermos of tasty soup were waiting for me.

Starting to get the feeling my mother was up to something.

Clambered into the dress. Toed on the shoes.

The *concierge* called to tell me my car was there.

So. Mother thought I might bail on her.

Hilarious.

And yet, given how much I hated society stuff, a predictable risk management strategy.

ALEXANDRIA BLAELOCK

The driver was waiting in the foyer.

9

The Royal Hotel is one of the oldest hotels in town. Renovated a couple of years back.

Presumably upgrading the fixtures to modern standards and tastes while refreshing its period charm.

I still find it slightly surprising that someone somewhere makes modern versions of antique toilets and wallpapers.

A porter opened the car door and offered a hand to help me out.

While I adjusted the dress, he opened the hotel door and ushered me through.

On the one hand nice.

On the other, his subservience made my skin crawl.

I wasn't the kind of self-important person who felt doors should be opened for me.

The whole hotel seemed taken over by the dinner.

Exquisitely dressed and coiffed women impersonated birds of paradise.

The birds and flowers.

And to go with them, men in White Tie with their fitted suits lightly padded in the shoulders and a surfeit of sewn bow ties.

Honestly, it's not that hard to tie a bow tie. Dad's not good at much, but even he can tie his own tie.

I felt conspicuous standing in the hotel foyer. Most often I'm sneaking around the edges of things, so standing in a crowded hotel foyer dressed conspicuously to the nines was out of my comfort zone.

Starting to feel a little dizzy, hornets buzzing in my stomach.

Either that or something in my supper didn't agree with me.

Then again, people aren't usually trying to kill me.

Took a deep breath and held it in for ten seconds.

Then grabbed a glass of champagne from a passing waiter and sculled it. Hid a burp behind my hand as I exchanged the empty for a full with the next.

Much better service than buses and policemen; waiters everywhere.

With my back to the wall, I skirted the edges of the preening, caterwauling throng.

Trying to find Mother.

And get a grip on why she'd sent me here in the first place.

Passed a board with the seating allocations, then reversed back to find out where I was sitting.

I rubbed my temple.

I was allocated to a table with Taipan himself.

Wondering how Mother'd swung that.

Hoping she wasn't matchmaking.

Did he know I was coming?

Checking the list twice more to find she wasn't even at the event.

Annoying.

Why here?

Why him?

Why now?

Maybe he wouldn't recognise me. Hell, I hardly recognised me.

Brown was not on the list, but that didn't mean she wouldn't be there.

Unofficially.

Like me.

Some guy announced it was time to move into the function room for dinner.

I sidled away from the door, and half concealed myself behind a pillar to watch as the guests flocked through the function room door.

Surprisingly swiftly.

It's not as though they were likely to miss the food service.

Did that mean they were all here for some other purpose?

I'd just watched a movie with a black-market auction partly hidden in a charity auction...

I wiped my clammy hands across my belly, hoping I wasn't staining the bodice. I wasn't clear on whether the dress had to be returned.

Or whether I wanted to let it go once the night was over. Always handy to have a "good" dress.

The foyer emptied out, and I was almost the last one to go through.

As far as I could tell, no sign of Brown

Shortly after, the doors shut with a solid boom.

It reminded me of another movie where the monsters took their human disguises off after the doors shut.

Managed not to turn around to look at the doors.

In any case, the people I could see remained people.

As you'd expect.

Just milled around in a smaller environment and got louder as the alcohol started to hit.

The room itself seemed a fairly standard function room. Parquetry dance floor in the middle, white linen-clad tables for eight as far as the eye could see.

The usual arrangement of hundreds of forks and glasses and linen table napkins.

No obvious places to hide.

No obvious places to escape.

There wasn't much point delaying the inevitable.

I moved through the room, nodding at people I knew.

Who stared back.

Understandably, they didn't recognise me, but I couldn't help feeling offended. I'd grown up with these people.

The only seat left at the table was next to Taipan.

I shook my head, just my luck.

On the one hand, not in his direct sight, on the other within talking distance, and on the third, I couldn't ignore him.

He was attractive enough, though I'd recently decided he was definitely not my type...

Filled out his suit with muscle, not padding. The same herbal cologne he was wearing when I hung under his desk.

I sighed.

Aware that I'd been sighing a lot since I got myself into this mess.

Might as well get it over with.

"Good evening," I said to the table as I pulled out my chair.

"Bubba Gee!"

A stifled squawk came from the seat beside me. I ignored it.

"Uncle Ben!" I left the chair and moved around the table to exchange kisses.

Uncle Ben isn't a blood relation; he went to University with Mother.

He wouldn't let me call him Mr Adams, she wouldn't let me call him Ben, so they compromised on Uncle Ben.

I've adored him forever because he always squatted down to talk to me at my eye level.

"Bubba Gee?" Taipan asked.

I glared at him, but Uncle Ben laughed, "when she was very young we used to call her Baby Georgia, but all she could manage was Bubba Gee. God, she was adorable."

"What happened?"

"She grew into an adorable young lady of course," he said winking.

I rolled my eyes.

Then glared at Taipan.

"How do you know Georgia then?"

I opened my mouth to cut him off Taipan got there first, "I ran into her at a friend's place."

The literal truth, but I'd met him three times in three different "places" over the last couple of days, so which meet was he thinking about?

Also, fairly sure not yesterday.

They looked at me to continue the story. I shrugged as I walked back around the table to the empty seat, "wasn't it at that charity thing last year?"

"Was it? I don't remember that," Taipan said with a smile, "but I remember yesterday."

Uncle Ben whooped.

"I expect you meet a lot of people in your line of work," I said. "I wouldn't've thought you could remember anyone, let alone when you met them."

"I would definitely remember adorable you."

The table laughed.

Thankfully another waiter arrived and started filling glasses with red wine.

The man next to Uncle Ben nudged him with an elbow and leaned across to talk to him.

And the six other people moved on as I returned to my seat.

I suppose they assumed we'd come together.

"It took me five hours in a salon to look this good."

Taipan leaned his elbow on the table and turned to look at me, "only five?"

If he'd been an inch closer...

I'd've sent him to the moon - Honeymooners style.

The situation was uncomfortably reminding me of my monthly romance movie marathons.

He reached a hand toward me, "I love what you've done with your hair."

I brushed his hand aside with a karate block.

Trying to figure out how to make him stay away from me.

"I've done what you asked."

He nodded, pulled back and smiled, "good job."

As if I was that snarling ball of fluff back at Brown's place.

"So now our business is over?"

"Of course."

"No backsies."

He rubbed his chin as he looked at me, "well you could come work for me."

My jaw dropped.

"You got in and out of my apartment without anyone knowing, and I could use someone with your talents."

I grabbed the wine glass and sat back in my seat.

I knew Brown had set the bomb but had Taipan sent his clean-up crew to Gran's place? To, well, get "rid" of the problem?

"Hundred grand plus benefits," he suggested.

It was a sum that made my eyes water, and for a moment I considered it. Looking over my glass at Taipan, trying to work out what was going on inside that thick skull of his.

But you can't take a company from nothing to a multi-billion-dollar industry if you can't control your face when you're negotiating.

I admit it.

I was tempted. No more living in my office or struggling to make ends meet.

But.

As crass as it sounded, I valued my independence.

And I was also annoyed.

Obviously, he was lowballing me, and I had no idea what I was worth.

"No," I said. "You can hire me by the hour plus expenses. Just like every other contractor."

He laughed and leaned back in his chair.

Why was that funny?

Ah.

Prostitutes with hearts of gold.

I rolled my eyes again.

"What's your fee then?"

I figured it had to be extortionate to put him off. "Five grand an hour, and don't be forgetting the expenses."

"Done," he said, pretending to spit in his hand.

Too late to ask for more money, though I had the idea it wouldn't matter how much I asked for.

I had no choice but to shake his hand.

Touched his hand to find he had in fact spat in it.

How disgusting.

Next thing he'd be telling me he didn't worry about written contracts because his word was his bond.

Managed not to break his fingers while shaking his hand.

But.

I couldn't really complain about it either; if I'd still had an office, a couple of hours would see the arrears paid off and cover the rent for several months to come.

Doh!

Maybe it was time to grow up and get real. There were no Robin Hoods in modern times.

Which reminded me; I still had to come up with the money for my shitty ex-landlord.

Taipan didn't let my hand go but leaned toward me.

His breath ticked my neck as he whispered in my ear, "I need your help to recover something else from the same person."

"Uh-huh."

Oh my god, I just couldn't get away from her!

She would quite literally be the death of me, I was sure.

"She's taken some highly confidential information, and I need it back."

Was that the "photos" I'd picked up from his office, or something else? For that matter, was it the envelope he'd already had me hide in her apartment?

"Is that something we've already exchanged or something else?"

He snorted under his breath, "I didn't know you had a sense of humour."

"Oh for fuck's sake, stop flirting. Just tell me what it is you want."

Even do-gooders snap at times.

"Temper, temper."

"So help me, if you want to live, you'd better get on with it."

"Okay, okay. Keep your shirt on."

I laid my hand on his leg, fairly close to his crotch, and dug my fingers into the muscle. With my nicely manicured and purple polished fingernails.

He winced.

Though I'm fairly sure he only did it to be polite.

He did, however, get back to business.

"She's downloaded the ledgers. I don't know how she accessed the secure system, and I don't know how she's storing it, or who she's planning to give it to."

"Was this before or after you installed her downstairs?"

"After," he said.

"And your security guy has investigated all her internal contacts with anyone who has access."

"Yup."

"No obvious leads?"

"No."

"Recently enough that she probably still has it?"

"Yup."

"And your guy's had her followed to make sure she hasn't already made a drop?"

"Yup."

I rolled my eyes, though he was too close to see it.

"Okay, to sum up; she's downloaded a file, you don't know when or how, where she's storing the data, or for whom?"

"Er... Yes."

"So how do you know she's actually the culprit?"

"She told me."

"She told you?"

"Yeah. She came right out with it and told me. And when we checked the logs, the file was accessed and a copy taken."

My heart wavered.

Just because she'd said she took it didn't mean she had. It could've been a misguided bid for attention.

Or someone else did it and she just claimed it was her.

By which logic, was she actually the one who'd blown up my office?

"And you're confident your security guy is working for you, not someone else?"

He rubbed his jaw. "Of course. He's been with me since the beginning!"

I wondered if he was too close to the guy to recognise it was time to pull out. Was it Confirmation Bias and he was just ignoring the evidence to the contrary?

"And you've had him quietly investigated since I broke in?"

He didn't say anything.

Or was it like the Sunk Cost Fallacy? He'd invested so much time in the relationship he wasn't prepared to let it go.

"I see. You should consider at least doing a cursory security check by and independent third party to ensure he doesn't have any issues like gambling debts or other potential sources of blackmail. Even something as seemingly innocent as a new girlfriend."

"Can't you do it?"

"She blew up my building, the day I broke into your place. I don't have a computer to do it with."

"I'll get you one, we'll consider it an expense."

I decided to let it go because I had Mother's laptop for the moment. And it wasn't worth arguing about.

"What about the girl? How did you meet? Did you have her investigated?"

"Sure. Met her at a function like this, had her investigated, she's all clear."

"And your guy did the checking."

"Yeah. Why?"

Was it possible I was making too much of this?

Was she a criminal mastermind, or was she a honey trap?

For that matter, why are they named after sweet things? Sugar babies too. Is it because too much of a good thing will likely kill you?

I was debating whether to ask for danger money when I heard an outraged scream.

"I knew it!"

I thought I recognised the voice.

Leaned over to look past Taipan's head.

Sure enough, it was Brown.

Standing on the dance floor.

Dressed in slim jeans and a stained t-shirt.

Not guest. Not staff.

So, how did she get in?

And more to the point, was she there for Taipan or for me.

Probably him seeing as she was likely to know his movements some time ahead.

And I didn't know I would be here until I got here.

"You just can't keep it in your pants, can you?"

Yup, definitely him.

She took a few erratically mapped steps towards him, unsteady on her feet, probably drunk.

Or at least under the influence of some kind of intoxicant.

The room fell silent as the guests turned to look at her.

I scanned the faces, looking for something that might indicate who'd arranged her arrival.

Some avid, some horrified, some distasteful.

Nothing obvious, on guests or staff.

Taipan leaned back to see what was going on. Tensed up as if he was planning something.

Still had my hand on his leg. Applied the fingernails to make him stay down.

Her eyes locked on mine.

She twisted to face me.

"You," she roared, and pulled some kind of handgun from the back of her pants.

Definitely not a revolver.

Should've seen that coming.

She trained it on me. Right-handed.

Wavering as she tried to focus.

I stood up.

Set my half-empty wine glass on the table.

Picked up the cloth napkin.

She closed one eye.

Wavered some more.

Stepped slightly back for better balance.

Brought her left hand up to support her right.

I watched her body as she tried to still herself enough to take the shot.

At the point she looked about ready to fire...

I cracked the napkin out to my left.

Making a sound like a bull whip.

Almost as good as a fan.

She turned her whole body to her right.

The shot went wide. Almost instantly chipping moulded plaster off the ceiling.

Thankfully not an automatic.

The room gasped collectively.

But remained in their seats.

No attempt to flee.

No attempt to help.

No attempt to disarm the fucking psycho.

The problem with fancy dinners for rich fucks is that they all expect someone else to take care of problems.

None of the staff paid enough to consider intervening.

Brown frowned and refocused on me.

Sadly, she did not throw the gun at me.

Just shot again.

Still wide thank god.

The only thing left was to rush her and hope she couldn't get her shit together.

And someone would call the cops.

I walked around the table.

The gun followed me.

The shot clipped my shoulder.

Just a graze.

That god dammed fucking hurt.

And sent a rivulet of blood running down my arm.

Wasn't really prepared for that.

Tried not to look at it.

Or feel it.
Dropped into a crouch to reduce my target size.
Clutched at the probability of eighty to ninety-five per-
cent survival.
Crouch ran toward her.
She aimed again.
Dropped into a sliding tackle.
Took her legs out from under her.
She cried out.
Fell in an untidy heap.
Threw myself on her.
Held her flailing gun arm.
Felt something hot slide into my lower abdomen.
On my left side.
She'd got a fucking knife!
Well, technically I had it.
But where the fuck did that come from?
Blanked for an instant with the pain.
She pulled the knife out.
Stabbed me again.
If I didn't do something I would die.
She raised her head.
I took a deep breath.
Gritted my teeth.
Head butted her.
Fucking slammed it into the parquetry with mine.
Couldn't tell if she'd lost consciousness.
Pulled the gun out of her hand.

Slung it across the dance floor.
Forgot not to pull the knife out.
Clutched the wounds and rolled on my back.
Brown reared up and was on me.
Legs pinning my arms to my body.
At least she was keeping the pressure on my wounds.
Hands around my throat.
Squeezing.
Her blood dripping on my face.
What the fuck were the guests doing?
Gritted my teeth.
Pulled my knees up.
Feet to the floor.
Turned my face as far as I could to the side.
Bucked my hips.
Threw her forward.
She let go of my neck.
Took a deep breath.
Gritted my teeth again.
Pulled my arms loose.
Grabbed her right arm.
Held it tight.
Stepped over her right foot.
Rolled over.
Sat up between her legs.
Forcing them off the ground.
Pinned her hands to her chest.
Took another breath.

A gun wedged itself between us.

Pointed at her.

Let her hands go.

Slithered off her.

Flopped to the ground.

Took another deep breath.

Groaned.

Bikini clad ladies strolled around my head with their infernal signs. Taipan, two. Brown, two. Foul mouthed Private Investigator Georgia Garside trumps all.

I passed out.

10

I woke up. Opened my eyes and then clamped them shut again.

Outside them, it was really bright.

My throat hurt. My guts hurt more. I was thirsty.

And cold.

And tired.

Tried opening my eyes again. Blinked, then opened one eye.

I was in a hospital room. Sunshine streaming in the window, reflecting off the white walls and ceiling.

A whiteboard placed on the wall facing my bed told me what my name was, and that I had multiple abdominal puncture wounds and bowel surgery.

The handwriting was atrocious, but I suppose they didn't have time to write neatly.

Or take classes in medical hieroglyphics to frustrate the rest of us.

A tv hung from the curtain rail around my bed, off at the time, but with a tiny green light to let me know it was ready when I was.

Through an open door, I could hear people walking with carts, fragments of conversation, and the hum of air-conditioning.

Diagonally across the room, a blue door with a toilet sign made me want to pee.

Not a Pavlovian thing, though I suppose Mother trained me to go whenever I found a facility.

So, I looked around, working out how to get there.

I was sitting more or less upright in a hospital bed.

Couldn't see a call button, but I did see a drip fixed into the back of my left hand. The stand was a little way from the bed and a little behind me. A blue box with a countdown was attached to it.

Plus, a finger pulse monitor on my right hand and a blood pressure cuff on my right arm.

And a nasal cannula with scratchy prongs scratching my nostrils. The gas hissed faintly as it travelled up my nose.

Two tubes ran out from under the covers, draining into bags hanging off the left side of the bed.

An empty rolling table was pushed to the wall.

A warm, happy sensation engulfed me, and I went back to sleep.

The next time I woke, I went through the inventory again. It didn't seem anything had changed.

Marginally annoyed there wasn't a clock, but at the same time, glad to be free of the incessant ticking.

Still had the idea I needed to pee, perhaps more so.

I tried to move my legs toward the edge of the bed but barely got started before the pain stopped me.

Concentrated on wiggling my fingers and toes until the pain went away.

Gritting my teeth, tensing my arms, trying to slide my legs further towards the edge of the bed.

Should I call out?

They like you to pee after surgery don't they?

Arms wobbling, tried to move a leg again. The pain was almost unbearable. For a moment I thought I'd pass out with it. But I'd convinced myself I was desperate to go.

I panted for a moment, relaxing my jaw and arms.

Rested up for about a hundred years

Then worked my legs the tiniest bit further towards the edge.

Rested. Worked a little further.

Then a nurse arrived.

"Probably best not to move too much right now darl."

"I need to pee."

She leaned over to check the bags hanging off the bed, "the catheter's draining well, do you feel like you really need to go or just think you should?"

Thought about it, "probably just habit. But I am thirsty,"

"Then I'll get you some water. Sit tight."

Several minutes later she came back with an opaque yellow jug of water that rattled with ice and a clear plastic glass with a straw in it. She put them on the mobile table and pulled it closer to the bed.

She half-filled the glass with water and offered it to me. Happily, she caught it as it fell through my fingers.

Then drew the table across the bed and put the glass where I could lean and drink from the straw.

It was hard to feel so feeble. If Brown came in, I wouldn't be able to defend myself.

The nurse was fiddling with the blue box when I asked if she'd been brought in as well.

"Not here in surgical, but perhaps sent to another ward?"

I grunted.

Surely there'd be guards or something outside her room if she was here, so I was probably safe.

Just have to get well enough to discharge quickly.

She handed me a small red buttoned device connected to the drip.

"Okay. So I've taken the morphine off automatic, so when the pain gets too much, just push the red button. You don't have to worry about overdosing as the prescription is programmed in."

I nodded.

"Are you comfortable?"

"Not really."

She raised the head of the bed a little higher, pulled another control over the bed frame and down my right side. Handed it to me and pointing at the buttons, explained the controls, "head up and down, feet up and down, overhead light, tv on and off, volume and channels, and this one for a nurse."

"I'll just do my observations and leave you to rest," then took my blood pressure, temperature and checked the pulse monitor was still attached.

She noted the details in a file she'd taken from a rack hanging on the end of my bed.

"Now, have you passed wind yet?" she asked.

"I'm sorry? Passed wind?"

"Yeah, have you farted?"

I snorted and then winced, "farted! I get it now. No. I haven't passed wind."

She made a note.

"On a scale of one to ten, where ten is the highest, how much pain are you in?"

"Ummm. Seven maybe."

"Okay," she said writing that in the file as well, "you should probably give yourself some morphine now then. I'll

leave you to rest, and don't forget to call if you need anything." She dropped the file back into the rack.

"Thanks."

I pushed the button.

When I woke again, Gran was there.

"I hear you were quite the hero last night."

"Was it only last night?"

"Uh-huh."

I reached out for the water.

Gran stood up to push the table further up the bed and pour some water into the glass.

Going by the way it sloshed I guessed a few hours had passed since the time I pushed the button.

"What time is it?"

She looked at her watch, "nearly four o'clock."

It felt weird, and I was a little creeped out by how long I'd been out of it.

"How is your house?"

"It'll be fine. The police said there's been a few tit-for-tat drive-by shootings recently and they must have just got the wrong house."

"Yeah, I suppose that's possible."

She smiled, "anything's possible."

"I still think it's related to a case I'm working."

"Shame you lost everything in the fire then, isn't it?"

I nodded. I was trying not to think about that until this was over. If it ever was.

"Anyway, I was watching you sleep for a while, and I want to catch the train home before rush hour starts."

"You're still living there?"

"Why wouldn't I be?"

"Oh, I don't know. Just seems weird."

She shrugged, "it's my home. The Police did all their investigating already and gave me permission to start repairs."

"Then I suppose that's a good thing."

She collected her things together, "is there anything you need for next time?"

"You could find out where my things are."

She stood up and opened and closed a few cupboards, then pulled at a locked drawer.

"Nothing here, aside from whatever's locked in there. The Police probably took your clothes for evidence anyway."

"The Police?"

"Of course. The woman assaulted you."

"Oh yeah, I suppose she did."

She gave me a kiss, "if you think of anything, let me know and I'll bring it in tomorrow."

"You don't have to come tomorrow!

She patted my hand, "of course I don't, but I'm going to anyway."

And then she pushed my button, "I'm sorry, but you look like you're..."

85

13

I think we'll just gloss over the next few days because I don't believe anyone wants or needs the details.

Which are disgusting.

So, if you're that kind of pervert, you can go read a different book.

And we'll pick up again once I'm safely ensconced at Gran's place.

To be fair, Mother did offer (more than I'd expected) but I couldn't bear the thought of her fussing around.

Or her complaining about Dad.

But we'll pick it up having tea (and sticky ginger cake) on Gran's verandah.

14

When Gran joined Mother and me on the verandah, she was carrying a large tray laden down by the enormous aluminium pot wrapped in a tea cosy she'd knitted, a selection of mismatched cups, saucers and plates, some folded kitchen towel, and a fresh-baked ginger cake.

Mother took it off her and carried it to the table, laid out the cups and saucers and poured the tea while Gran cut generous slices of cake.

I took a sip. Hot and strong, just the way I like it.

I sighed and stretched my legs out to catch the sun.

In case you wondered, I was wearing one of Gran's old dresses. The one I found least objectionable.

There can be no pride when you have nothing.

"I brought you the laptop," Mother said. "I know you were barely in the flat, but couldn't you have made an effort to keep it tidy? I walked in and it was like a bomb had gone off."

"Janice," Gran hissed, nodding her head towards me

Mother made a strangled sound as she remembered my office had been blown up, but I laughed.

Literally laughed until I cried.

89

"There, there," said Gran, patting my back.

"I'm sorry," I said, "I guess it's all just caught up with me." I filled my mouth with cake.

"I'm sorry too," Mother said, wonder of wonders, "I could have put that better."

I nodded, chewing.

"But I am disappointed you disrespected my things."

"The worst I did was leave my clothes on the floor in the bathroom, and my dishes in the sink."

"Then how would you explain furniture upended on the floor, drawers emptied, torn cushions on the couches?"

"I can't. Is it possible you were broken into?"

She gave me a look, "security is *very* good there."

I just looked at her like the dumb arse I thought she was. Impossible I could have sprung from her womb.

"Now, now," said Gran, "give the girl a break. She's been through a rough couple of weeks."

Mother sniffed and turned her head away.

I took another bite of ginger cake.

"Oh by the way," Mother picked up her bag, "you dropped this at mine when you were there the other day," and offered me Brown's fountain pen.

I had an idea who turned over her apartment and why.

I put the plate on the table and wiped my hands down my dress before I remembered who owned it. I glanced at Gran and she narrowed her eyes but didn't say anything.

I grabbed a piece of kitchen towel and found the pen didn't work.

I unscrewed the barrel and a tiny thumb drive fell out.

Mother and Gran leaned in closer to see what it was.

Then Mother handed over the laptop.

I had the idea it belonged to Taipan, but I had to check.

I turned the laptop on and slipped the drive in.

"I'm not sure you guys should be looking at this, there may be consequences."

"Pfft," said Gran, "they've already shot my place up."

Mother snorted, "plus they've trashed my place."

The drive held dozens of folders. I clicked one at random, and opened a ledger spreadsheet.

Opened another folder and picked a document that looked like some kind of legal matter.

With a space above Taipan's name to sign.

I closed the files and folders down and withdrew the drive.

"Well, I guess we know what they were looking for now."

"And why they broke into my flat."

Not actually an apology, But I'd take it.

"Can't say I know how I'm going to write the invoice."

"What invoice," asked Gran.

I put the drive back in the pen, and dropped the pen on the table. Then took a sip of tea.

"I asked him for five thousand dollars an hour plus expenses," I waved the teacup in the direction of the pen, "for its return."

Gran laughed, and Mother said, "that's my girl."

15

A gratifyingly large sum hit my bank account.

Plus Taipan paid for my medical care and added a second sum labelled "Workers Compensation" on my bank statement.

He also repeated his offer of employment, and I repeated my refusal.

He said he'd get in touch with his "special" cases.

I really hope he doesn't. I don't want to come up against his next enemy.

Or the sugar babe.

Brown was arrested for espionage or something and a bunch of other charges like reckless endangerment, and attempted murder.

She was sent to prison for twenty-five years with a non-parole period of eighteen years.

So I don't need to worry about her for a while.

I've pencilled a note in my new diary to see what she's up to in fifteen years.

There was enough money to buy some new clothes, pay the bond and a couple of months' rent on a new place, but I didn't bother looking right away.

I needed a few months to rest and rebuild my fitness and stamina first.

And Gran's place was comfortable. She refused to take any money, but I made sure to buy plenty fripperies and treats for her.

Taipan lost the election.

Nothing to do with me.

Just got caught in a sex scandal. One of his previous sugar babes "leaked" some intimate details.

Big brain, little brain.

Though he might have got away with that if he had divested his business interests instead of giving them to his nephew.

Or at least placed his assets under the control of a third party.

In an attempt to make peace with Mother, I agreed to attend twenty-six functions over the next year.

So, every two weeks I get dressed up and follow her to Gallery openings, gala dinners and balls.

It's not exactly torture.

Now and again, we run into Taipan. I think she chooses those functions on purpose so she can watch me squirm.

The biggest surprise was Gran buying the land my office used to be on. I'm not sure whether she traded the Garside name, or kept the plans modest, but she got the plot cleaned and the building constructed in record time.

And on the top floor, there's an office with a small apartment where I live and work.

I manage the building, and she gives me a small wage for that.

I still have my Private Eye business.

But that's another story...

THE END

As a small token of my thanks for reading...
Please enjoy 10% off everything (excluding shipping)
at alexandriablaelock.com
with the code bbkten.
Turn the page for some ideas where to use it...

RELATED MERCHANDISE

MORE RELATED MERCHADISE

Foul-mouthed. Ex-contortionist. Bomb survivor.

Georgia Garside is back!

Hunting a missing woman through Melbourne's streets.

Unravelling the truth to reveal something much darker.

A quirky fast-paced mystery you won't see coming.

One good turn deserves another

Ellie Porterfield is not one of THE Porterfields though she works in high-end fashion at their department store.

When a severely beaten man collides with her at a bus stop she calls an ambulance and renders first aid.

Is drawn further into a web of danger and deceipt that could cost her life.

But could it shed light on her troubled past as well?

Welcome to Wilkinson's

I'm afraid Mr Hall's running a little late, can I get you a tea or coffee while you wait?

No?

What if I tell you about some of the recent cases we've been involved in?

Yes?

Then get comfortable and settle in for a wild ride.

Felicia Clarke; influencer.

Old Fashioned. Fiercely independent.

Encourages others, but treads her own path.

Dead, but fondly remembered.

By some.

Australian author Alexandria Blaelock writes mostly fantasy and mystery.

She's appeared in the Stringybark Anthology *Crowd Surfing*, *Pulphouse Fiction Magazine*, and *Ellery Queen's Mystery Magazine*.

She's also written five self-help books applying business techniques to personal matters like getting dressed, tidying up, and feeding friends.

Discover more at alexandriablaelock.com.

Be the first to know!

Just sign up to receive my Insider Updates so you can stay up to date on my writing, get advance notice of new releases, discounts, free eBooks and much, much more in my monthly communiqués.

At alexandriablaelock.com/insider-updates/